Travis
and the Tropical Fruit

Illustrations by Dynamo

EGMONT

95% of the paper used in this book is recycled paper, the remaining 5% is an Egmont grade 5 paper that comes from well managed forests. For more information about Egmont's paper policy please visit www.egmont.co.uk/ethicalpublishing

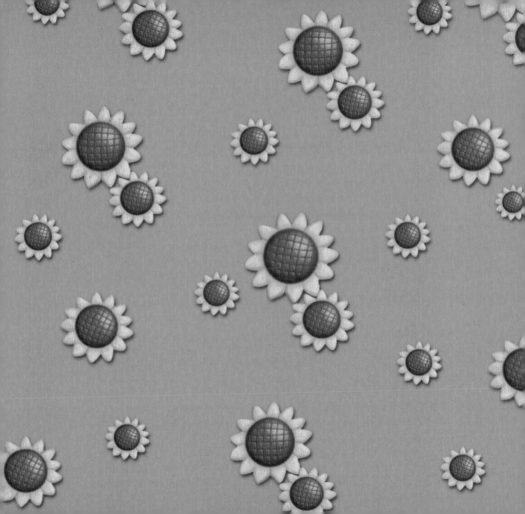

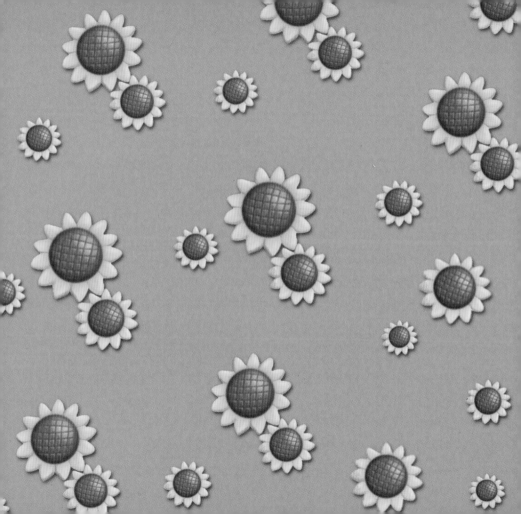

EGMONT

We bring stories to life

First published in Great Britain 2008 by Egmont UK Limited
239 Kensington High Street, London W8 6SA

HiT entertainment

ISBN 978 1 4052 4110 6

1 3 5 7 9 10 8 6 4 2

Printed in Great Britain

When Mr Beasley says he wants to grow pineapples in Sunflower Valley, Travis offers to help. But things go wrong, and Travis and Spud make a real stink!

Travis the tractor had come to visit his friends in Sunflower Valley.

"Farmer Pickles has gone to Bobsville today," said Travis. "Got any jobs for me?"

"No, sorry, Travis," said Scoop. "But there'll be a job somewhere! You just have to look for it!"

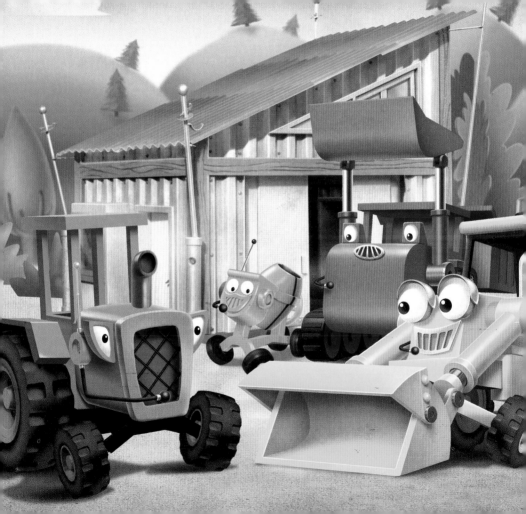

Meanwhile, Mr Beasley was showing a special box to Bob and Wendy.

"My pineapple seedlings have just been delivered!" he smiled, opening the box.

Bob and Wendy were puzzled.

"Sunflower Valley's not hot enough to grow pineapples!" said Bob. "They grow in tropical weather!"

"But the box says they need planting straight away!" Mr Beasley frowned.

"Don't worry," said Wendy, kindly. "Let's look up pineapples on the Internet."

Wendy found a picture of a pineapple pit on her computer and showed Mr Beasley.

"I've never built one of those!" laughed Bob. "It looks like your pineapples are going to be heated by horse manure!"

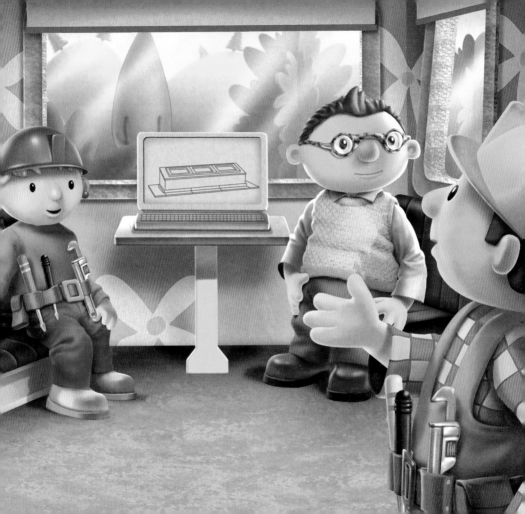

Bob went to the yard to tell the team.

"What's horse manure?" asked Muck.

"It's, erm, horse poo," said Bob. "It sounds silly, but it will heat up the pineapples and make them grow!"

"I moved a whole load of horse manure at Farmer Pickles' farm yesterday," said Travis. "I'll fetch it and be back before you know it!"

The farm was far away in Bobsville, but Travis got there quickly. He loaded up his trailer with the horse manure.

Just then, his talkie-talkie began to crackle. It was Bob!

"Take your time, Travis," said Bob. "The pineapple pit isn't built yet ... and manure is a bit smelly!"

"Ha, ha! Erm, OK, Bob," said Travis.

Travis decided to unload the manure in a clearing beside the Bentleys' eco house, until Bob needed it.

Near by, the Bentleys and the Sabatinis were having a picnic.

"Goodness me! Whatever's that smell?" said Mr Bentley. "We can't stay here. Quick, pack up the picnic!"

"Oh, deary me!" worried Travis, and he trundled away with the trailer of manure.

The next day, Mr Beasley went to see how Bob and the team were getting on. They had been very busy building the pineapple pit.

"When we put the manure in, it will heat up the soil and make the seedlings grow!" Bob told Mr Beasley.

"These glass covers will keep them warm and the pong inside!" Wendy laughed.

Travis had taken his trailer to Scarecrow Cottage. He needed Spud to help him move the manure.

"My parsnip nose! What a whiff!" said Spud. He disappeared inside the cottage and came back wearing a funny mask.

"Ta da! Spud's wearing Farmer Pickles' special mask for cleaning out the pig sties!" boomed Spud, through his mask.

Soon, Spud and Travis had made a plan.

"The big pile of manure makes a big stink, but lots of little piles will just make lots of little stinks," said Spud.

"No one'll notice a thing!" agreed Travis.

So Spud shovelled the manure into sacks, then Travis took them away to hide all over Sunflower Valley.

A few days later, it was time to add the manure to the pineapple pits.

Travis and Spud told Bob about how they had stored it in the sacks. "We hid them all over Sunflower Valley," said Spud.

"Oh, dear!" chuckled Bob. "How will we find them again?"

Just then, Mr Bentley arrived. "Don't worry," he said. "I'll soon sniff them out!"

And that's just what they did! Spud, Travis and Mr Bentley searched behind bushes, trees and buildings until they had found all the sacks.

"Wow!" said Travis. "What a clever nose you have, Mr Bentley!"

They took the sacks to Bob, and he and Spud shovelled the manure into the pits.

Before long, the pineapple pits were as hot as a tropical jungle!

Months passed while the pineapples grew, until finally they were ready to eat.

Mr Beasley invited everyone to taste the tropical treat, and it was delicious!

"Horse manure! That's the secret," he laughed. "I'm going to grow all sorts of tropical fruit next – mangoes, bananas …"

"Oh, no! You know what that means, Travis," groaned Bob. "More manure!"

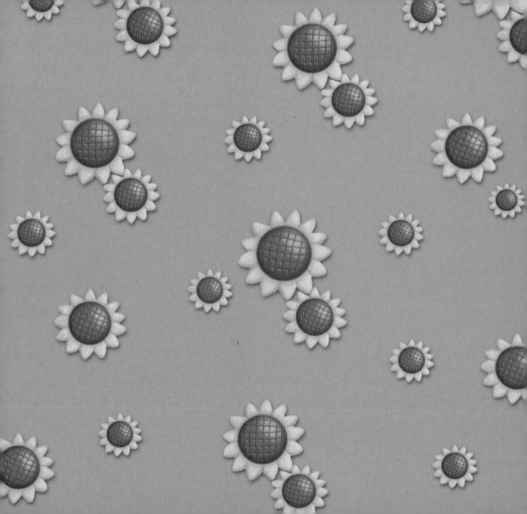

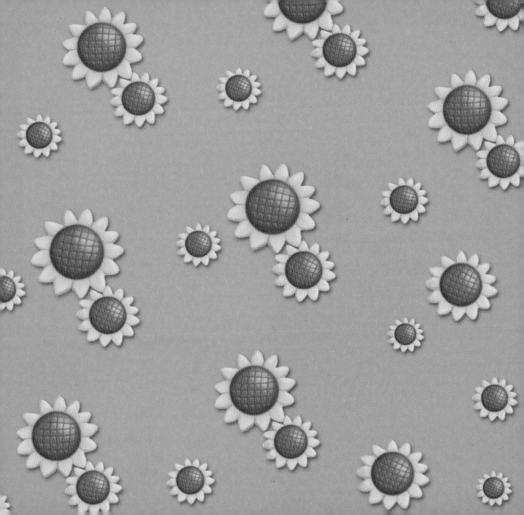

Start collecting your Bob the Builder Story Library NOW!

RRP £2.99

1. Bob and the Big Plan — ISBN: 978 1 4052 3142 8
2. Dizzy and the Talkie-Talkie — ISBN: 978 1 4052 3143 5
3. Scrambler and the Off-road Race — ISBN: 978 1 4052 3144 2
4. Wendy and the Surprise Party — ISBN: 978 1 4052 3140 4
5. Roley and the Woodland Walk — ISBN: 978 1 4052 3750 5
6. Benny and the Important Job — ISBN: 978 1 4052 3748 2
7. Sumsy and the Sunflower Spill — ISBN: 978 1 4052 3747 5
8. Muck and the Machine Convoy — ISBN: 978 1 4052 3749 9
9. Travis and the Tropical Fruit — ISBN: 978 1 4052 4110 6
10. Lofty and the Singing Stars — ISBN: 978 1 4052 4111 3
11. Scoop and the Bakery Build — ISBN: 978 1 4052 4108 3
12. Spud and the Funny Trees — ISBN: 978 1 4052 4109 0

My Bob the Builder Story Library is THE definitive collection of stories about Bob and the team. Look out for even more terrific titles coming soon!

A fantastic offer for Bob the Builder fans!

1 BOB TOKEN

NOTE: Style of poster and door hanger may be different from those shown.

£1 STICK COIN HERE!

In every Bob the Builder Story Library book like this one, you will find a special token. Collect 4 tokens and we will send you a brilliant Bob the Builder poster and a double-sided bedroom door hanger!

Simply tape a £1 coin in the space above and fill out the form overleaf.

To apply for this great offer, ask an adult to complete the details below and send this whole page with a £1 coin and 4 tokens, to:

BOB OFFERS, PO BOX 715, HORSHAM RH12 5WG

☐ Please send me a Bob the Builder poster and door hanger. I enclose 4 tokens plus a £1 coin (price includes P&P).

To be completed by an adult

Fan's name:
....

Address:
....

....

Postcode:
....

Email:
....

Date of birth:
....

Name of parent / guardian:
....

Signature of parent / guardian:
....

Bob the Builder

Ref: BOB 004